WATCHER
AT THE
WINDOW

BY CATHERINE STORR

ILLUSTRATED BY JUDITH LAWTON

LONGMAN

This book is part of
THE LONGMAN BOOK PROJECT

General Editor Sue Palmer
Fiction Editor Wendy Body
Non-fiction Editor Bobbie Neate

PEARSON EDUCATION LIMITED
Edinburgh Gate, Harlow, Essex CM20 2JE, England
and Associated Companies throughout the World.

Text © Catherine Storr 1995
Illustrations © Judith Lawton 1995

First published 1995
ISBN 0 582 12221 X
Sixth impression 1999

Printed in Singapore (PH)

The publisher's policy is to use paper manufactured from sustainable forests.

CHAPTER 1

That week in the spring, everything happened too quickly for Robert to remember.

On Monday, he'd been told he'd been picked for the team that was to play in Saturday's match. He hadn't believed it at first. He was fourteen, thin, wiry, not built big and broad like most of the other players. Playing in a match was something he'd dreamed about, but hardly ever thought possible. He'd said, "Me?" incredulously, and Mr Harris had said, "Yes, you. I've been watching you and you've come on a lot lately. I don't say it'll be permanent, mind you. Might have to reorganise things later, but I'd like you to have a go at it. All right?"

Robert found it quite difficult to say, "Yes, sir." And "All right" didn't express a thousandth part of what he was feeling. He couldn't wait to tell everyone. His friends first, then when he got home, his brothers and his mum. She would be pleased because he was over the moon, but she wouldn't really understand all that this meant to him. Johnny and Clive would and they'd sun themselves in his reflected glory. Dad would have known exactly how much it meant to be picked for the Rugby Club team at his age. It had been Dad who had taken Robert to his first match, had taught him almost everything he knew about the game, who had coached him on the scrubby bit of ground near the bridge, bullied him, even, to get his footwork right, showed him how to tackle, how to outwit his opponents. It was terrible not to be able to share this triumph with his dad. For a moment this thought made Robert almost sad.

That evening, after supper, Robert said, "Mum?"

"What?"

"Have you got Dad's address?"

"What do you want it for?" She was immediately suspicious.

"I'd like to tell him about me getting into the team."

"I don't know where he is just now."

"You must have got his address somewhere," Robert said.

"I don't suppose he's still at the last one he gave me."

"I could try it, couldn't I?" Robert was getting angry. "There's nothing wrong with my wanting to write to my dad."

His mother sniffed. Robert knew that sniff. It said, I don't know why you should want to bother with your dad. He doesn't bother much with you, does he?

She'd said it often enough, and it hurt. Dad had gone off on a job abroad for six months, he'd said, but that was three years ago, and in that time he'd only come back once, and then not to stay. "I'm better away from your mum. We shouldn't ever have got married, that's all there is to it. If I tried living here again I'd probably commit murder one day," he had said then. Robert had said, "What about me? - Us?" he had quickly amended so as not to sound too selfish.

"You'll be all right. I'll be sending money to your mum. More than I'd be able to if I stayed in this hole."

Robert wanted to say all sorts of things. That it wasn't a hole, it was his home town, and that bits of it were beautiful and he loved it. That he wanted Dad to stay. That he'd miss him horribly, and that having Mum couldn't make up for not having his father. But he wasn't used to saying things like this, so he didn't say anything, and the next day his dad left again. It was now more than two years since he'd visited them. "Dad sends you money, doesn't he? Don't you know where it comes from?" Robert now said to his mum.

"It's a money order. Comes from his savings account."

"Doesn't he write to you ever?"

"What about? No, he doesn't."

"He sends postcards sometimes. Last one was from America," Johnny said.

"That was months ago. Anyway, I've never had an address for him in America," Robert's mum said.

"There must be some way of writing to him!" Robert said.

"I'll give you the last address I've got. It was up in Scotland or somewhere. Diving for treasure, I suppose," Robert's mum said.

"Oil platforms," Johnny said. He was always the best informed of the family about world affairs.

The address did not look promising. It was on the back of a very tattered envelope and Robert saw from the postmark on the front that it was at least six months old. However, before he went to bed that night, he wrote to his dad to tell him the news. "I wish you'd come to the match, it's on Saturday the 16th at two o'clock," he wrote. He didn't really believe that his dad would get it in time, but all the same he posted it on his way to school the next morning.

CHAPTER 2

It was a wonderful week. He was a hero at school, he'd begun to feel like a hero to himself. He wanted Saturday to come quickly, but he also wanted to spin out the days in between so that he could enjoy the looking forward and the admiration of his friends who weren't lucky enough to be playing, but who would come to the match to cheer.

Afterwards he couldn't remember much about the day itself. There'd been frantic preparations in the morning, he'd been too excited to eat anything, he'd been angry with his mum for trying to persuade him. He'd sworn at her, something he didn't often do, then felt bad about it and had rushed out of the house without saying he was sorry or goodbye. And then? He thought he remembered going out on to the pitch. He

was told afterwards that they'd played for twenty minutes or so before it happened.

Perhaps it was lucky he didn't remember more about the accident. Had there been pain at the time? There'd been plenty afterwards. The only thing he remembered quite clearly was opening his eyes and seeing a room he'd never seen before. All white, and strange people standing round a bed. He was lying on the bed. He tried to say, "What ... ?" but no word came out.

After that there was a long, long time of almost nothingness. Almost, because during that long blank night there were moments when he woke and other moments when he dreamed, but couldn't afterwards recall what he'd dreamed. And then a slow, a very slow, return to the ordinary world, when he knew where he was and who he was and what was happening.

But it wasn't his ordinary world. It was a hospital. He was in bed, and couldn't get out of it by himself. Nurses came and took his temperature, shook up his pillows, scolded him and joked with him, and washed him. (Oh, the shame!) Doctors came and poked at his legs and his body and his arms with pins and with feathers. They asked, "Can you feel that?" and "Does that hurt?" and "Can you move this?" In a prison of rage and despair, Robert answered their questions sullenly; but if he tried asking them anything, they didn't give him clear, sensible answers. "When can I go home?" "How long will I be like this?" and at last, frantic, "Will I be able to walk again, ever?" To this the doctors said things like, "Early days yet, old son," and "You're in a hurry, aren't you?"

Robert's mother came every day. Robert knew there was something he ought to be saying to her, but he didn't know now what it was. He asked her the same questions, but she didn't know any more than he did. All she could tell him was that during the match – that great match – someone had tackled him and brought him down and that in the fall he'd hurt his spine. That was why he couldn't feel his legs, couldn't move them.

"Who was it?" Robert asked, ready for murder.

"I don't know," his mother said.

"Someone must know. Did you ask?"

"Mr Harris said it was better not to know. It was an accident, Robert!"

An accident! Some stupid clot tackled you so that you were in hospital for weeks and lost the use of your legs! "When am I coming home?" Robert asked next.

"The doctor said in another month or two. Then you'll have to come back here for treatment. Exercises and … other things."

That wasn't too bad. He knew enough about injuries at sport to realise that you had to teach your muscles to work properly again. He said, "Suppose I'll have to learn to walk again, like a baby?" Then he saw his mother's face. "Mum! What's the matter?"

"Haven't they told you? You'll have to be using crutches when you come back home."

"Crutches! You mean just at first?"

She didn't answer that. "And they're letting us have a wheelchair for when you go out. We'll have to keep it in the passage downstairs, so that you can get out in it. Upstairs you'll have to make do with crutches." Their flat was on the first floor, over the ironmongers in the High Street.

"You mean it's going to be a long time?"

"I don't know. The doctor didn't say."

"For ever? D'you mean I'm never going to be able to walk again?"

"They didn't say that." But he could tell from her face that they had not said anything encouraging.

"What did they say?"

"Nothing. I don't know. They don't tell me." His mum was crying now. It was as bad as it could be. He was going to be in a wheelchair for life. He was a cripple. He wished he had died.

CHAPTER 3

He wished it more than once during his weeks in the hospital. Weeks? He was there for more than three months. It was the end of August when he was finally brought home, in an ambulance, and carried like a baby into the front room of the first-floor flat, which was now to be his. His bedroom. His world.

"You'll be able to see out into the street," his mother said.

"What's the use of that? There's nothing to see."

"People. The shops. You'll see plenty of people you know."

"I'm supposed to spend all day looking at other people walking around, when I can't?" Robert said, hearing himself being difficult and, in a nasty way, enjoying it.

"Rob, I'm sorry. You know there isn't anything I can do about it. I can't stay at home with you. I have to go to work." His mother worked every day at the hairdressers in Church Street. 'Top Dressing', it was called. What a silly name!

"I'm not stopping you."

After she'd gone, Robert didn't look out of the window on purpose. What did she think he was, an idiot, who would sit and stare at a busy street, contented with nothing more than movement? He looked at the pile of books she'd brought the day before from the local library. He didn't want books. He hated everything and everyone. He wanted to be himself again, active, good at games, good enough at school work, unthinking, unworried. It wasn't fair that he should be here, stuck in a chair, hardly able to get himself to the WC, dependent on other people all the time. He hated old Mrs Emmet who came in to get his dinner in the middle of the day. He hated Johnny and Clive for being able to walk into the room and out again, on their own useful legs. He hated his mum for not being able to help him and he hated his dad for not being there. He hated the world. He hated God.

Because he was so miserable, he was also horrible. He sulked. For days he wouldn't answer questions, wouldn't speak to his mum or to Johnny and Clive. He had no choice but to go to the clinic three times a week for his exercises and physiotherapy, but when he was there he did as little as he could to help himself. The girl who was in charge of his treatment, Frankie, did her best, but he knew she found him impossible, and he was pleased. She was small, but strong; he had to admit that she had surprising power in her skinny arms and narrow back. She put him through his exercises, once a week she took him into the pool and tried to make him move his useless legs. Robert, in a savage mood, deliberately sabotaged all her efforts.

She was giving him a lesson on using his crutches, when she suddenly said, "Why don't you listen? You aren't even trying!"

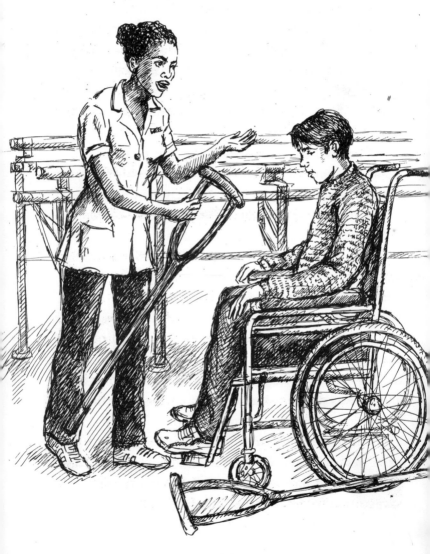

Robert didn't answer.

"Don't you want to get better? Don't you want to be able to get around by yourself?" she asked him.

"What's the use?" Robert said.

"Well, if you want to be a useless lump all the rest of your life, I suppose that's your affair," Frankie said.

"I'm never going to be able to walk again, am I?" Robert said.

"You could if you'd really try. You've got to keep the crutches straight, like ... "

"That's not proper walking!"

"It's a step towards it. You'd be surprised what a lot people on crutches can learn to do."

"Running and jumping? Wheelchair marathons? It's stupid!"

"No, it isn't! It's doing something positive instead of giving up."

"Well, I'm not going to do anything like that."

"You don't know how lucky you are. Suppose you'd been paralysed in your arms as well as your legs? I've had patients worse than you," Frankie said.

"It wouldn't make much difference," Robert said, convinced that no one had had worse luck than he had.

"That's what you think. Now, I'm going to give you another exercise to do at home. I want you to do it ten times every morning and ten times every night. I'll write it out for you so you don't forget it."

She wrote it, and Robert did not forget, but he also did not do the exercise. When he went back for his next visit and she asked him how he'd got on, he told her he was not better. He saw that she was angry and upset at his total lack of progress, and he was pleased. 'That'll teach you to tell me I'm lucky. I'm not. I've had rotten bad luck, now you're getting it for a change,' he thought.

When he was at home, things were no better. He noticed presently that his mum had stopped trying to please him by cooking his favourite meals, or by bringing him comics and books to read. She came and sat with him in the evenings after she'd finished work, but they didn't talk much. The TV set had been moved into Robert's room, and generally it was he who chose the programmes. His mother, exhausted, generally slept for most of the evening. Johnny and Clive were sometimes there, but as often as not Robert was the only one looking at the screen with hot, angry eyes.

CHAPTER 4

Surprisingly, Johnny was the only one of the family who wouldn't be put off by Robert's deliberate bad manners. When he wasn't at school he spent time in Robert's room. "What d'you want to do your homework here for?" Robert growled, and Johnny said, "It's quieter in here." All the news of what was happening in school, in the town, reached Robert through Johnny; not that Johnny told it to him directly, but he'd tell Mum or Clive, speaking rather loud, just outside the open door of Robert's room. It was often Johnny who carried in Robert's meals, and brought his own plate too, balanced it on the chest or the back of a chair, and ate, standing up. If Robert asked why, Johnny always had a good excuse. "Don't want to see Clive again today, him and me had a fight." "Mum's on at me about those shoes I lost. She won't try that in here."

At first, Robert resented this companionship, but soon he came to accept that whatever he said or didn't say wasn't going to drive Johnny away, and he came to take his presence for granted. He even allowed Johnny to take him out of the house in the wheelchair. It had to be after dark, he wasn't going to have people looking at him and being sorry for him.

So some evenings Johnny wheeled him along the back streets to the end of the common. This was the rich part of the district, locally known as 'Millionaire's Row'. The wide roads were bordered by large houses standing separate from each other, surrounded by big gardens. Some of these were protected by high walls, but there were others that had only low walls or iron railings, and you could see the beautifully arranged flowerbeds, the tennis courts, often a green pool. There were older trees here, and he could see poplars whispering to each other in a gentle wind, or, if the weather was rough, the chestnuts and the oaks

whipped their top branches about as if they were trying to shake off the leaves that were only just beginning to turn copper and brown. Robert didn't mind seeing trees moving like that; it was different from seeing people walking and running, children hopping and skipping. The trees were like him, they were rooted in one spot. They were not rivals. Sometimes then, for a short moment, he felt different. Not happy, not reconciled to his crippled state, but almost as if there just might be things he could enjoy. But the feeling didn't last. By the time they were back home again, and he had to be helped upstairs, to get undressed and got into bed, he was raging again. And being as disagreeable as he knew how.

He felt it as a personal insult that the summer had almost gone. He had hardly seen it. He'd had plans for what he was going to do on long warm evenings. He'd thought of asking Anthea to come with him to the Saturday market by the canal, where you could eat instant food like filled pancakes or stuffed baked potatoes while you wandered round the different stalls and looked for something that you wanted and that you could afford. Anthea had said she'd never been there, her mum thought it wasn't safe for her to go alone. Which was nonsense: Robert knew lots of girls who went there alone and nothing bad happened to them. But it suited him if Anthea's mum felt that she needed protection. And then, he'd thought, they could walk along the side of the canal, which wasn't madly interesting in itself, but would give them an opportunity to talk and he'd be able to see if he wanted to go out with her again. He wasn't at all sure what he felt about her. She wasn't wonderful to look at, like Sidonie Frost or Marian Dewey.

Sidonie was lovely. She was not just the pin-up girl of his year, she was the pin-up girl of the school. Everyone knew that Ted North, the captain of the football team, had taken her out. Sidonie could go out with any boy she chose to. She wasn't particularly bright, she came more or less average in her schoolwork, but what did that matter when you had her looks? He'd been mad about her for nearly two months last year; every time he'd shut his eyes he'd seen the curve of her cheek as she pushed her bright hair back from her face, something she did all the time. Then, suddenly, for no reason he could guess at, he'd stopped being interested in her and just got annoyed at the way she fiddled with her hair.

Marian had been different; he still liked her, and he still thought she was nice to look at, gypsyish, with heavy dark hair and large dark eyes. But she was either terribly shy or terribly stupid, he hadn't been able to decide which. She never spoke except to answer questions, and then it was only with a "Yes" or a "No", or, worse still, she'd say "I don't know" or "I don't mind". "Shall I get you an ice cream, Marian?" "I don't mind." "Shall we go to the pictures?" "I don't know." "Which would you like to see, *Hurricane Hugo* or *Alone on the Prairie*?" "I don't mind." At last he'd actually said to her, "Look, do you want to go out with me or not?" and she'd said, "I don't mind," and that had been the end.

Anthea wasn't like that. She wasn't a great talker, not in class, anyway. But she did know her own mind. Robert had heard her telling off one of the other girls for laughing at poor stupid, clumsy Diana, who never stood up for herself. "You're mean! You're horrible! She can't help how she is, it's something that happens to some people. You might have been born like that. How'd you like it if everyone laughed at you when you couldn't manage something?" she'd shouted. That had been brave of her. There was a whole group of girls in her class who teased Diana, hiding her shoes or her books or her swimming things so that she was even later for lessons than usual. Then Diana would cry and they'd shout "Crybaby!" at her and make her worse than ever.

Now he hadn't a chance of asking Anthea to do anything. He didn't imagine that she would be interested in sitting by a wheelchair. What could they find to talk about? Nothing happened to him, he hardly saw anyone, he couldn't ask her out. The thought of her pushing him along the street in his chair made him sweat with embarrassment. He hadn't let anyone except Johnny take him out in the chair yet. He couldn't bear to be seen sitting in it, helpless like a baby. But a baby would grow up and learn how to walk and to be like everyone else. He, Robert, wouldn't. He had nothing to look forward to. He might as well be dead.

He had meant to take no interest in the street below his window. He despised it. But since he had nothing else to look at, he found that, against his resolve, he began to recognise patterns in what went on there. At the end of his first month of imprisonment, he knew that at eleven o'clock on Tuesday and Thursday mornings, the long crocodile of primary school children would be on their way to the local swimming pool, carrying bags and satchels and backpacks containing their swimwear and towels. An hour and a half later, they were there again, going in the opposite direction, their hair still damp. He couldn't help noticing that the visit to the pool had made most of them more alert, or perhaps just hungrier for their midday meal. They walked fast on the way back, and there was more laughing and teasing. The young man who always accompanied them had difficulty in keeping them in order. Robert remembered feeling like that himself: he remembered the delicious feeling of cool skin which yet seemed to glow from inside after swimming. But that had been when he had come half chilled out of the water and run to get warm again, like those kids. Now he had to be hauled out of the pool by Frankie's strong arms and warmed by sitting near the radiator. Robert scowled as he thought of this.

He began to become familiar with the routine of the High Street. There were the big delivery vans with the hydraulic platforms which came to deliver goods to the supermarket on the other side of the road. He saw the trolleys of loaded cartons being wheeled into the shop, and later he saw the empty boxes stacked outside. The first van arrived before he was up in the morning, but he knew that from eight o'clock onwards vans were arriving about every half-hour throughout the day. He had, too, a good view of the security van that often stood outside the bank directly opposite his window. That van was there at different times on different days, and it was much quicker than the goods van. Men in safety helmets marched from the road into the bank at a brisk trot. Robert wondered if they carried guns. He wondered what they would do if someone tried to intercept their progress across the pavement.

But nothing as exciting as that ever happened.

CHAPTER 5

Gradually, as the days went on, he found that he was beginning to recognise different people as they went about their daily business of shopping and walking their dogs and pushing their prams up and down the High Street. There was the old man with a small dog on one of those retractable leashes which was constantly getting wound round the rubbish bins and lamp-posts. The old man never seemed to notice what the dog was doing until he found that he couldn't continue his walk because the dog had tied him to some immovable object. There were a great many young women pushing prams and baby buggies. They often stood and talked to each other in the middle of the pavement, getting in the way of other, busier shoppers. There were various old ladies with sticks, who hobbled slowly past, clutching baskets or bags. There was a young blind man who went tapping along with a white stick. At the pedestrian crossing on the corner, he always stopped until some passer-by would lead him across. Sometimes he stood there for minutes before anybody offered to help. Robert felt a sort of sympathy for him; there was another person who couldn't manage life on his own. He wanted sometimes to open his window and call out "Why doesn't someone take him across the road?" But he never did. His sympathy wasn't strong enough to

break his determination not to have anything to do with all that busy life going on in the street. If he couldn't share it as an equal, he wouldn't get involved.

Occasionally he found that his curiosity got the better of him, and he once or twice asked his mother if she knew the people he watched. More often than not she didn't. She worked too hard and too long every day to have time for making or visiting friends. But because of being in the hairdressing salon, she could identify some of the people. "Who? A very tall girl with fair hair right down her back and a baby in a purple suit? That's Molly Feast, comes into the shop every Wednesday for a shampoo and manicure. Plenty of money, husband's in business, I don't know what sort." "Yes, that's Mrs Morecombe, that old lady. Lives somewhere just off the High Street. She's in every other week for a shampoo and set. A talker, she never stops. A bit touched, I'd say, she tells you stories about what she used to do when she was young, and I'd swear not half of them are true. Poor old thing, I think she's lonely. Lives by herself and needs someone to talk to." But Robert's mother did not know the old man with the dog, nor the blind man, nor the bag lady who dawdled along the pavements carrying a full plastic bag in each hand and smiling to herself as if she knew a secret she didn't mean to share with anybody.

"There's a lady drives up to the bank in a Rolls. Do you know her?" Robert asked.

"I don't know anyone with a Rolls," his mother said.

"She might come to have her hair done in your shop," Robert said.

"If she goes about in a Rolls, it's more likely she'd go somewhere grander than 'Top Dressing'. What's she look like?"

Robert didn't know how to describe her. "Small. Not as tall as you. Her hair's brown. No, lighter than that. It's reddish."

"What sort of clothes does she wear?"

"I don't know. Nothing special." Robert wasn't interested in the lady. It was the Rolls that fascinated him. "She doesn't drive herself, she's got a driver. In a cap. He's black."

Robert's mother did not know the lady with a Rolls and a black driver. Surprisingly, it turned out that Johnny did.

"That's Mrs Braithwaite. Her husband's a millionaire. Lives in Millionaire's Row."

"How'd you know?" Robert asked.

"Eddie's in my class at school. It's his dad drives the Rolls."

"Have you seen it close to?"

"It isn't ever at Eddie's. I've been there. The Rolls is kept in the garage where Mrs Braithwaite lives."

"Has Eddie been out in it?"

"He has once. His dad had to take it to the garage and Eddie went with him."

"Will he ever ask you to go in it with him?"

"'Course not! His dad shouldn't really have taken him that time."

The next time that Robert saw the Rolls he studied the driver. Eddie's dad was young and tall and he wore a grey uniform with a flat grey cap. Robert didn't see much of him, only a glimpse until he got out of the driver's seat and opened the door at the back to allow Mrs Braithwaite to get out; then he stood by the car, occasionally flicking a speck of dust off its gleaming black paint, until she came out of the bank, and he held the door for her to get in. This happened regularly once a week, at half-past ten on a Tuesday morning. Robert imagined the lady saying to the bank clerk, "I'll take a thousand pounds this morning," and the clerk counting out the notes for her. He wondered what she spent them on. He wondered how much Eddie's dad got paid for driving that beautiful car. He asked Johnny to find out, but Johnny said he couldn't ask that sort of question and, even if he did, Eddie wouldn't tell him.

These were only a few of the hundreds of passers-by that Robert saw every week. There were many whom he saw only once and didn't remember. There were many others who went past so often that he only noticed when he failed to see them. Without meaning to, he found that he had given some of them names. The old man with a dog was Mr Moon –

because of the dog, and because he was so absent-minded, mooning. The blind young man was Peter, he wasn't quite sure why. The bag lady was Mrs Bags, and a tall, thin, elderly man, who was often hanging around the High Street, but who only ever bought anything except a newspaper and a carton of milk, was Scorcher. In Robert's imagination he had been a secret agent when he was younger. He had a way of looking around him suspiciously, as if he was afraid of being followed or taken by surprise in some way, which was exactly how Robert expected a retired spy to behave.

There were whole days when he didn't appear at all, so what was he doing then? Writing his memoirs? Or trying to find another job? Perhaps visiting another country and offering his undercover services there?

Robert would not have admitted it, but there were minutes, sometimes even a half-hour, when he was sufficiently interested in what he observed out of his window to forget his situation. Of course these gaps in time did not last. Most of the day he was bored and angry and impatient; but though he did not know it, he was not quite as angry or as bored or as impatient as he had been in the summer when his imprisonment had first begun.

CHAPTER 6

He was astonished when Sidonie came to see him.

Even at the time when Robert had admired her, it would never have occurred to him to ask her to go out with him. She had been one of those unattainable prizes, like playing for England, or a Porsche, or a video camera, that feature in your daydreams but are nowhere near your real life. So when Johnny, very flushed and hardly able to speak, came into his room and said, "Sidonie Frost's come to see you," he didn't believe it until he saw her.

It was lucky that he was looking reasonably respectable. He wished he hadn't been wearing his old dressing-gown, and that the room had been a bit tidier. But Sidonie didn't seem to notice. She came right over to him and said, "Hi! Mind if I visit you for a while?" and sat down on the chair the other side of the window, looking at him.

Robert didn't know what to say. He'd hardly exchanged a word with Sidonie since they'd been in primary school. Then he'd teased her and insulted her and ignored her in the way all the boys teased and insulted and ignored all the girls. After they'd gone on to the secondary, the great barrier had fallen between the sexes. They were no longer children, they had begun to feel themselves almost young men and women. The boys kept to themselves and the girls did the same, like armies encamped on opposite sides of the field. And then, one boy and girl would detach themselves from their camps and go off together, followed by other pairs, until they were almost as mixed as when they'd been little. Except that the pairs were constantly changing, and feelings ran high. Much higher than when the worst disputes had been about Brenda's green trainers or Mervyn's spectacles, or who had told tales about Jason's rude limerick.

Robert said, "It's nice of you to come," and wondered why she had.

Sidonie said, "No, really, I wanted to."

Robert wanted to ask why, but he couldn't. There was a long pause. Then he said, "Would you like some tea?" His mum had said that when he had visitors he should always offer them a cup of tea as long as there was someone else in the flat who could get it.

Sidonie said, "Yes, that'd be great." She did not offer to find the kitchen and make the tea herself, as some people did. Robert pushed the button of the bell which was taped to the arm of his chair, and Johnny looked round the door.

"Sidonie wants some tea," Robert said. He knew he wasn't doing this at all well. He was too much embarrassed to feel at ease. He knew he should have asked for the tea differently, not as if Sidonie had demanded it.

"Cup or mug? Sugar?" Johnny asked, and Sidonie said, "A cup, and sugar, please." When it came, she drank it in very small sips. Well, at least it took up the time, during which Robert didn't have to think of anything to say.

"What do you do all day?" she asked at length, when the cup was empty.

Robert was tempted to say, "Nothing. What do you expect?" Instead he said, "I don't know. I read a bit. Watch telly."

"You poor boy!" Sidonie said.

There didn't seem to be an answer to this, and there was another silence. Then Robert said, "How's school?"

"Ghastly. I can't wait to leave."

"What'll you do when you leave?"

"I'm not sure. I might be an air hostess." She stopped as if she expected Robert to comment.

"I expect that'd be interesting," he said, feebly.

"But what I'd really like would be to be a model." This time there was no doubt. She was waiting for him to make some remark. He supposed she wanted him to say, "That'd be great!" But he didn't feel that it would be anything like great. He knew that some girls liked dressing up and showing off their clothes, but the idea of spending your life doing that and posing for photographers in extraordinary attitudes seemed a daft way of spending your time.

He started to say, "Would you really like ...?" but Sidonie interrupted him. "I've been told I look right for a model," she was saying. She turned her head so that Robert saw her profile against the wall behind her chair. He realised that he had missed a cue. When she'd said that about being a model, he should have said something about her looks. But now he was too embarrassed to think of the right comment.

Sidonie hardly noticed. She said, "I've got just the right measurements and my hair's right, too. It's ever so easy to manage. I wouldn't have to have it dyed blonde like some girls do. It's natural."

Robert remembered how they'd teased her when she was a small girl for having white hair. It hadn't been white then, of course, but silvery blonde. Now it was a shade darker.

"Of course I'd have to learn how. I'd go to a model school in London. You have to learn how to walk, you know, and how to hold a pose."

"Hold a what?" Robert said.

"A pose. For the photographers. They tell you where to stand and you have to be able to understand exactly what they want."

"Wouldn't you get bored doing that all the time?" Robert suggested.

Sidonie opened her beautiful eyes wide. "Bored? Of course I wouldn't. You get to travel to the most fabulous places. Egypt and America and India and all over. And the money's great. I read the other day about a model who was earning sixty thousand a year. And she wasn't a top model either."

Robert said, "Wasn't she?" He felt that his stock of conversation had run out. Perhaps it was lucky at the moment Sidonie looked at her tiny gold wristwatch and said, "Ooh, it's late! I'll have to go. It's been lovely talking to you, Robert. I'll come back some time, shall I?" She was gone before Robert had time to answer this question, or even to think whether he wanted her to come back or not.

CHAPTER 7

It was October. The mornings and evenings were dark and in the daytime the sun hadn't much strength. Robert had never before had to spend whole days just sitting still. He sometimes found that without noticing that he wasn't warm enough, he could become chilled right through, after which it took a long time to get warm again. His mother produced an ancient shawl made of squares knitted in different coloured wools. "My Aunt Betty made it. I used to put it over you when you were in your cot. It'd keep off the draught from the door."

"Mum! No! It's horrible."

"It's beautifully warm."

"But it looks ..."

"I like it. It's nice and bright. Just try putting it round your shoulders."

"No! I'd feel like an old bag."

"Well, put it over your knees. They say if your knees are well covered, that keeps your feet warm too."

"I'm all right," Robert lied.

"No one's going to see it," Robert's mum said.

"I said, No! Take it away. I can't stand it!" Robert said, and then felt ashamed that he'd shouted at her.

"I wish I could afford to let you have the electric

fire in here all day, but it costs the earth," his mother said.

"I'll be all right. You can bring me that blanket off my bed. I'll put that round me if I get cold."

"Or you could wear your anorak."

He didn't want to wear the anorak. His mum had found it in an Oxfam shop last winter, a bargain, practically new, the envy of his friends. He'd worn it to go sledging on the common, he'd strutted round the school playground in the cold snap in January. He had looked good in it, and knew that he had. It was somehow wrong to have to wear it in this poky room, just to try to keep warm. It deserved better than that. But he knew that his mother was trying not to annoy him and he knew too that the expense of an extra fire would be a worry she could do without. So he said, "All right. If I get cold, I'll wear the anorak."

He thought they'd come to the end of the conversation, but instead of going off to the kitchen to cook their supper, his mother was still there, standing first on one foot and then on the other, the way she did when she had to say something she knew he wouldn't like.

"Robert, I wanted to talk to you."

"You've been talking."

"About something else."

"Go on, then."

"Seriously. I went to see your school today."

"I can't go back!" Robert said. To have the people who'd been his friends, or, worse, his enemies, seeing him in the wheelchair, having to be sorry for him? He prepared himself for a fight.

"No, but you can't go on like this, not learning anything."

"I can read," Robert said, though he didn't think that *The Mystery of the Hollow Claws* was going to count as a textbook.

"Mr Gabriel says you could have a tutor."

"What's that mean?"

"Someone who'd come here once or twice a week and give you lessons. He'd set you homework, too. After all, your exams are supposed to be the summer after next."

"I won't be taking exams!" Robert said, in horror.

"Why not?"

"I'm not well enough. I've missed a term. I can't!"

"Mr Gabriel says you could catch up easily. He says you're clever."

"I'm not that clever," Robert said, determined not to be.

"You've got to think of your future," Robert's mother said.

"What for? I'm never going to be able to walk again, am I?"

"With your crutches?" his mum suggested.

"So what am I supposed to do with my crutches?"

"There are plenty of jobs where you don't have to walk around. You could learn about computers, Mr Gabriel says. You have to have your schooling. It's the law," Robert's mother said.

"I know the law says I've got to go to school if I can, but I can't."

"It's the law that if you can't get to school, you have to have lessons at home. It's no good being cross, it's all arranged. The tutor's coming to see you this evening to fix up lessons."

"Mum! I don't want –"

"I'm sorry. You'll just have to put up with it, won't you?" Robert's mother said, and Robert knew from her voice and the way she walked out of the room that it was no use arguing.

He was too angry about the whole idea to want his supper. He was pleased, in a disagreeable way, to see that this worried his mother, but she didn't spend long trying to persuade him to eat because, he realised, she was expecting this unwanted tutor to be ringing the front doorbell at any moment, and she didn't want to be caught carrying dirty dishes around. She tidied up his room as much as she could, while he sat in his chair in a white rage.

The tutor was a surprise.

Robert heard the doorbell. He heard his mother go down the stairs, slowly because she was always tired at the end of the day. He heard the front door open and he heard his mother's voice and two lots of footsteps coming up the stairs. His mother opened the door of his room and said, "Here's Robert." Robert looked for the figure he'd been imagining, though he hadn't quite made up his mind what that would be. He'd thought of an old man with grey hair and perhaps a grey beard, a retired headmaster like the one who had come to his school to talk to the upper forms about careers. Or perhaps it would be a younger man who couldn't keep order in school, so he'd take on this tutoring job, in which case he'd be sandy and weedy and have a high-pitched voice and would be frightened of everything. Robert had seen that sort of character on TV soaps. What he had never

imagined was that a tutor might be young and cheerful. Nor had he for a moment dreamed that it would be a woman. Coming in at the door after his mother was the tall young woman with fair hair and the baby that he'd got used to seeing out there in the High Street. Only this time she hadn't got the pushchair and the baby.

"This is Mrs Feast," Robert's mum was saying, and the tall woman said, "Hallo, Robert." Robert, without really knowing he was going to, said "Hallo" back.

"Would you like a cup of tea? Or coffee?" Robert's mum said.

"Not just now, thanks, Mrs Fox. I've got to get back home in five minutes. I left Jim with the baby," Molly Feast said.

"If you don't mind, I'll go and get finished in the kitchen," Robert's mum said, and left while Molly Feast was saying, "Of course. I just want to find out from Robert where we'd better start."

She sat down on the chair opposite Robert's and began to ask questions. Where was he in the school? Had he begun work for GCSE exams? What sort of maths had he done? Was he taking any languages? Did he know what the set books were for the English exams? Had he done any science? And Robert, who had started by feeling like an object under a microscope, being prodded and turned over by his examiner, found that he was answering her questions easily and without being made to feel stupid. He recognised that this Molly Feast was a professional. She wasn't out to make him feel small or to flatter him, she was just trying to discover what he would need from her. It took longer than the five minutes she'd said she had to spare, but by the end of a quarter of an hour she had found out what he was good at and where he'd need extra help. Robert had never been with a teacher who was so quick on the uptake.

When she got up to leave, he was almost sorry.

"I'll have to come in when I can. I expect you'd like mornings best, wouldn't you?" she asked.

"Don't mind. I'm here most times," Robert said.

"It'll depend who I can get to look after Ben," she said.

"Who's Ben?"

"My baby. My mum has him some mornings. I could generally come at this time, when Jim's back from work, but you'd probably find it harder to concentrate in the evenings. And anyway, I don't think Jim'd think much of coming home and finding me dashing out as soon as he's put a foot inside the door."

"So when ...?" Robert asked.

"I'll come and tell you next Monday evening, after I've spoken to my mum."

"I go to the hospital Monday, Wednesday and Friday mornings," Robert said.

"What time?"

"Half eleven."

"If I could get here at ten, I could give you an hour before you go. I expect you're pretty tired by the time you get back, aren't you?"

Robert agreed that he was. He could have said that he was generally cross too, but he didn't want to make himself out to be too difficult to this cheerful young woman. When she had gone, he was surprised to find that he was almost looking forward to seeing her again.

CHAPTER 8

When he heard the front doorbell, the next Monday afternoon, followed by steps and voices coming up the stairs, he expected that it would be Mrs Feast, come early to tell him when she'd be able to give him his tutoring, but when Johnny opened his door, and said, "Someone to see you," it wasn't his new tutor behind him. It was someone who hung back, reluctant to come through the doorway.

"Come on. He won't bite," Johnny was saying and Robert saw Anthea hesitating as if she wasn't sure of her welcome.

He wasn't pleased. He liked to be warned when visitors were coming, so that he could be wearing proper clothes, not his horrible old tartan dressing-gown. He liked to have the room fairly tidy. Above all, he liked to be sure that he wouldn't have to go to the bathroom during the visit. It was embarrassing to have to crutch his way there, clumsy and slow in front of visitors.

Anthea came a little way into the room and stood looking at him. Sidonie had swept in and sat herself down as if by right, and that had been easier to deal with. Now Robert said, "Why don't you come right in?" and realised that his voice sounded cross rather than welcoming.

"I'll be off, then," Johnny said, and disappeared.

"Why don't you sit down?" Robert said.

"You don't want to see me," Anthea said.

"Sit down, now you're here," Robert said.

She came nearer but she still didn't sit.

"I can go away again," she said.

Robert made himself say, "No, don't." But he knew he still was not sounding pleased that she'd come.

"Johnny said he thought you'd like to have people coming to see you," she said.

"I don't mind," he said, sounding just like Marian, and angry with himself for being so feeble.

"Are you mostly here by yourself all day? Or is your mum at home?" Anthea asked.

"She's at work most of every day."

"Isn't there anyone here with you?"

"There's Mrs Emmet, lives in the upstairs flat. She's sort of in and out. She gets me my dinner when my mum's not here." He didn't want to say that it was Mrs Emmet who helped him to get about the flat when he got stuck, which sometimes happened. She could be summoned by the handbell, which he was supposed to keep by him wherever he went. Once he'd rung it for what seemed like a hundred times, when she'd been out shopping, and he'd found himself left, sitting on the lavatory seat for nearly an hour, his crutches having fallen away out of his reach.

"You've got a wheelchair. I saw it in the passage

downstairs. Is it electric?" Anthea asked.

"No. Just ordinary. I can push it around with my hands, but it's a bore, I don't do it much."

"I've seen people in wheelchairs running marathons. Well, not running. You know what I mean."

Robert had seen them too, and he'd thought them pathetic. He said, "Stupid asses."

"Why do you think they're stupid?"

"It's pretending, isn't it? As if they thought they could really run, when they can't and they never will be able to."

"Well, I think they're brave," Anthea said.

"You think that's the sort of thing I ought to do?" Robert asked, disagreeably.

"Not unless you wanted to. I just don't think it's stupid to try to do things like that."

Robert couldn't imagine himself pushing his horrible wheelchair along the marathon route in front of thousands of spectators, all gaping at him and being sorry for him because he couldn't use his legs. And yet there was a part of him that wanted people to be sorry for him. He had a sudden, nasty feeling that Anthea had come to see him because she was sorry for him. She couldn't have come for the pleasure of his conversation. He said, "Did Johnny tell you to come here?"

"No. I asked him if he thought you'd like me to come."

"Why? Because you were sorry for me? Or did you want to see what I look like, now I'm disabled?" This was a word he hadn't used about himself before and he said it now, hating it and hating Anthea for hearing it.

"You don't look any different," Anthea said.

"But you're sorry for me?" Why did he have to ask this, when he didn't want to hear the answer?

"Of course I'm sorry —" she began, but he interrupted her.

"I don't want you to be sorry. I don't want anyone to be sorry for me. I'm all right ..." he said, furiously, and realised that he was very near bursting into tears. He couldn't go on. It was terrible. He couldn't cry in front of Anthea, and the hard ball in his throat prevented him saying any more. He had turned his head away from Anthea so that she shouldn't see his face which was red with the effort not to let the tears in his eyes trickle down his cheeks. He heard her say, "I'm sorry ... I mean..." Then he heard her walk towards the door. She said, "I think I'd better go now." The door opened and shut. He was alone.

Once she'd gone, he had no difficulty in repressing his tears. He was too angry to cry. He saw her cross the road beneath his window and walk down the street. She didn't turn her head to look up at him. Her back somehow managed to look sad, and Robert felt a moment's regret that he hadn't been nicer to her, then he comforted himself by thinking that she had been stupid. He didn't need her to be sorry for him, he didn't want to be pitied by anyone.

Out in the road he saw Scorcher, keeping close to the shopfronts as he always did, as if he did not dare walk in the middle of the pavement. Robert wondered whether he ever managed to cross a road, which involved stepping out into open space. Or perhaps he felt like Robert and didn't want to be looked at.

Johnny opened Robert's door and came in.

"Anthea gone? I didn't hear her go," he said.

"Went ages ago."

"She was funny about coming here. Said you wouldn't want to see her."

"Why'd she come, then?"

"Dunno. She seemed to want to."

"You didn't ask her to?" Robert asked, suspicious.

"Never thought of it. She came up to me after school and asked if I thought you'd like it. I didn't even know she was a friend of yours."

"She isn't. Not particularly."

"You like her, don't you?" Johnny asked.

Robert wouldn't answer this. He said, "Another time, tell me first. I don't like people coming when I don't expect them."

"Think she'll come back?"

Robert did not think so. He hadn't been welcoming when she'd first come in and at the end he'd been almost rude. He said, "No, I don't."

"What'll I say if she asks again?"

"She won't."

"What about Sidonie? Is she coming again?"

"No idea. Now shut up about them, I'm fed up with visitors."

But he was not sorry when Molly Feast appeared later in the evening. She was going to come in for an hour twice a week, Monday and Thursday mornings. "I'll set you work to do in between and we'll see how we get on. I guess you'll be surprised how much quicker you learn when you're the only pupil," she said.

This troubled Robert. Suppose he didn't learn quickly? She'd think he was stupid. He'd felt stupid in school sometimes, especially in German lessons, when he was supposed to understand what Mr Davidson was jabbering on about.

CHAPTER 9

The next day was Tuesday. If he hadn't had the big calendar hanging on the wall near him (he hated it, because all it had marked on it were the hospital visits) he'd have recognised the day from the activity in the High Street. The delivery vans were daily events, he didn't count them, but at 10.30 exactly the big black Rolls drew up on the opposite pavement and Mrs Braithwaite got out and went into the bank. She wasn't usually in there for long. Robert, without quite meaning to, had been timing her, and today it was the

regulation four and a half minutes. Now that he knew that her husband was a millionaire, he did look at her clothes with rather more interest, but he couldn't see anything about them that might have told him she was rich. She didn't wear fabulous furs, and as far as he could see she wasn't festooned with jewellery. She did wear very high heels and a very tight skirt, but then so did three-quarters of the girls in the top class at school, and they certainly hadn't much money.

He wished he could see inside the bank when Mrs Braithwaite was there. Did the manager come to greet her? Was she served before everyone else? What would happen if there was a bank raid? In his mind, Robert had often considered this possibility as a welcome diversion from the boring sameness of his days. He had often constructed the scene in which he saw a car draw up outside the bank, saw three masked men jump out and dash through the swing-doors. Then two minutes later the three came running out, holding bags and their sawn-off shotguns in their hands, threw themselves into the car and were whisked off. But clever Robert had taken the number of the car, and rung up the police station, and the robbers were caught and the money saved. Robert himself got a decoration and a reward.

No such luck. Nothing exciting like that would ever happen where he could see it.

Or perhaps an ingenious robber would tunnel

underneath the bank and come up into the vaults, like in the Sherlock Holmes story. He had asked his mum one day, "Do banks have vaults where they keep gold and stuff?"

"They have strong-rooms. People put jewellery and things there, to keep them safe," Johnny had said.

"How'd you know?" Robert asked.

"Read about it. Someone got into a strongroom and stole the lot."

"How much?"

"No one knew for certain. The people who'd put their stuff there didn't want to let on how much they'd lost."

"Why not?" Robert didn't believe this.

"Dunno. Something to do with not paying their taxes."

"What's taxes got to do with their jewellery?"

"Said I didn't know."

"What's a strongroom like, do you think?" Robert asked his mum.

"I don't know exactly. Very thick walls, I expect. Burglar alarms? And boxes all round, where people leave things they don't want to keep in their own houses."

"What sort of thing?" Johnny asked.

"I don't know. Jewellery. Family treasures ..." Robert heard his mother say, and his mind went off on a different tack. Things people didn't want to keep in their own houses could be anything at all, not just jewellery and family treasures. Clive had once brought home a snake and had meant to keep it in their bedroom, but their mum had got rid of it very quickly. Clive could have kept his snake in the bank's strongroom. How about a pet skunk? Or a tiresome old grandfather, like Will's, who wouldn't ever let the family do what they wanted in case it cost too much money, though everyone knew he had plenty?

When he came back from this fantasy, his mother was saying. "... family to know about. Like a will."

"I wish we had treasures we could put there," Johnny said.

"What for? They wouldn't do us much good, locked up in a bank."

"It'd mean we were rich."

Robert's mum sighed. She too wished they were rich.

"You could keep your jug there, Mum." The jug without a handle stood on a top shelf in the kitchen, and every week his mother put into it whatever she could spare from the customers' tips she'd had during the day. It was generally a year or more before she would take the jug down and count what was in it. Just now she was saving up for a new winter coat, but she doubted if she'd get it this year.

The next day was a Wednesday. He hated these mid-week hospital visits a little less than the Monday and

Friday ones, because on Wednesdays Frankie exercised him in the swimming pool. At the end of this session, he was surprised when she said, "You know you're not doing yourself any good. How are you going to get really better if you don't let me help you?"

"What d'you mean?" Robert said, suspicious and angry.

"As long as you just lie around like a log of wood, there's not much I can do."

"What's the use? I'm never going to be able to walk again, am I?"

"Who knows what might happen if you'd co-operate a bit?" she said.

"You don't know. You're only a physio. The doctor said I'd never get back the use of my legs," Robert said, enjoying being rude.

"All right. Be like that!" Frankie said. What seemed extraordinary was that what she had said made him feel worse. He might have expected that it would have given him hope and determined him to make every possible effort to recover. Instead he felt utterly miserable. Miserable, and also furious. Frankie had implied that he hadn't improved because he didn't try. She didn't know. What was the point of trying? The exercises she made him do were painful, and after months of doing them with her three times a week, he was no better, was he? What was the point of putting any effort into the stupid things? What was the point

54

of allowing himself to hope? He'd hoped enough in those first few days in hospital, and where had that got him?

He was exceptionally disagreeable to his family for the rest of the day.

It was the end of November. Robert's mother was kept busy with customers who wanted their hair and their fingernails to look their best for end-of-term and office parties. Clive was rehearsing for a Christmas school play. The weather was horrible, wet and cold, which depressed Robert's spirits more than usual. Last year his best present had been a football of his own; what would his mother give him this year? Books, he supposed, miserably; everyone thought that if you were disabled, living between your bed and a chair, you wanted more than anything to read. But he didn't. He'd never been a great one for reading, not like Johnny. Or she might give him a new pullover; she'd said several times lately that the old one he wore every day was wearing out. She'd even tried to find out what colour he'd like best. He'd been savage with her, said he didn't care, it might as well be black. She would never have thought of giving him books or a pullover if he hadn't had the accident. He'd have got something he really wanted. There had even been talk last spring of a secondhand bike. He groaned out loud.

CHAPTER 10

Nearly a week later, his mother gave him a surprise.

She came into his room, holding something wrapped in a piece of material that was quite different from anything that Robert had ever seen in her hands. It was a gaudy piece of silk. The colours were strange: orange, a sharp acid green, deep purple, dark crimson, peacock blue. They should have clashed horribly with each other, but instead they seemed to enhance each other so that the whole pattern glowed. Robert didn't have time to see more than this, before his mum was unwrapping the silk to show him what it had hidden.

She was saying, "I thought .... I knew you wanted ... It's a really good pair. Mrs Beckett said her husband ..." But he didn't hear the end of the sentence. He was gazing at what his mother was holding out towards him. A pair of field-glasses. Not a kid's pretend toy, not the stupid little things with mother-of-pearl casing like he'd once seen in the local antique shop, but the kind sportsmen used. The real thing. He put out his hand to take them.

"You're pleased?" his mother said.

"Mum!" He couldn't say more at first. He felt the weight of the thing. He raised it to his eyes and saw his mother's face ridiculously close. She had tears in her eyes. Robert realised suddenly that she had been unsure of his response, frightened even that he would refuse the gift, or take it ungraciously, as he did so many of the services she did for him. He said, again, "Mum!" Then, "How could you ...? I mean ... They must have cost a packet."

"I had some money saved," she said.

"Your coat!" he said. Then, with an effort, "You should have that coat, Mum. I don't really need these." But the feel of the field-glasses was heavy in his hands, and he loved them. To give them back now would be like taking the skin off his fingers.

"I don't need it. I wasn't ever sure I was going to get it this winter. I can't take those things back, anyway. Mrs Beckett really needs that money. She's selling off a whole lot of things that belonged to her husband and that aren't any use to her. When she was having her hair done this morning, she was telling me .... his collection ..... his clothes ..... not the cups he won, she's keeping them. But she's got to move somewhere smaller, and ..."

Robert wasn't listening. He'd put the binoculars to his eyes again, and was looking round the room. He saw things he'd never noticed before: a pencil mark on the wallpaper, a spider's web of tiny cracks in the paint of the door. He longed to pull back the net curtain and to lean out of the window to look up and down the street. But he knew his mother wouldn't allow that. He looked at her again, without the glasses. She was waiting for him to say something. He said, "Thanks, Mum. They're really great." Then, with an effort, "If I'd have thought of it, they're just exactly what I'd have wished for."

"I was going to give them to you for Christmas, and then I thought, why shouldn't he have them at once? You do really like them?"

That annoyed him. He'd said so, hadn't he? But he tried not to show his irritation. "They're fine. Now I'll be able to see everything that goes on."

"There's just one thing." But she didn't like to say what it was.

"What's that?"

"Don't let people see you're watching them. Keep

behind the net curtain. I wouldn't want the neighbours to think we were spying on them. You know how touchy some of them can be."

"You mean Walter?" Walter, who ran the take-away sandwich bar at the end of the High Street, was apt to imagine that people were talking about him. There'd been an almighty fuss when the government inspectors came round to look at the neighbourhood restaurants and cafés. Walter was convinced that someone in the town had reported his place as dirty. No one could convince him that the inspectors made routine visits, they didn't always wait for complaints, and for months after they had left (after reporting that conditions in his tiny shop were excellent) he eyed his patrons with suspicion, wondering which of them had betrayed him.

"He's not the only one. Just be careful, Robert, will you?"

"I'll be careful," he promised. But his mother had put interesting ideas into his head. With the binoculars he would be able to watch the comings and goings of everyone in the neighbourhood. He might discover more about them than they knew. If he'd been a bad character, he could have blackmailed them, though for what crimes or indiscretions, he didn't yet know.

CHAPTER 11

He could hardly wait, the next morning, to arrange himself at his watching post. Behind the net curtains, as his mother had stipulated. It was lucky that their lacy pattern had plenty of holes he could look through, though it needed careful arrangement to get both eyepieces of the binoculars free of the white threads. The street was crowded: it was Thursday, and people were doing their weekend shopping. There were customers in and out of the supermarket all the morning, and Jenkins, the butcher's shop, was busy, the red-and-white ribbons that hung over his open door were kept fluttering. The huge delivery van was parked outside the supermarket for nearly an hour; with the binoculars, Robert could read the labels on the cartons that were wheeled in. Not very thrilling. He could even read the labels in the butcher's window. 'Prime Topside – £2.80, Corn-fed Chicken, Organic Lamb Chops, Crown of Mutton. Rump Steak.' Boring.

The young blind man, Peter, came round the corner of Church Street and tapped his way to the pedestrian crossing. As usual he waited quite a long time before anyone offered to help him. Then it was Mr Moon who took Peter's sleeve and led him to the opposite pavement, where he was out of Robert's sight. Next he saw the bag lady, with different plastic bags today, one from Marks and Sparks and the other a very elegant one, dark purple and bulging. She was walking along the opposite pavement, smiling to herself, as usual. Sometimes she talked to herself and Robert wondered what she was saying; he wondered if he could learn to lip-read. But he didn't think that what Mrs Bags was saying would be very interesting.

It must be eleven o'clock, because here was the school crocodile on its way to the swimming baths. Robert was amused to see Mrs Bags get mixed up with the children. They flowed around her, like a stream round a wavering island, pushing her from side to side. With the help of the field-glasses, Robert could

see her puzzled expression, though she was still smiling. Presently the crocodile had disappeared, and Mrs Bags had gone out of sight in the opposite direction. The pavement was, for the moment, almost deserted.

Mrs Emmet opened Robert's door.

"Cup of tea?"

"That'd be fine."

"Biscuit? There's ginger and there's creams. Custard creams."

"Custard cream," Robert said.

When she carried in the tea, with the biscuit, already soggy because she'd let the cup slop over, Mrs Emmet saw the field-glasses.

"That's new! Where'd that come from?" she asked.

"My mum gave them to me."

"So you can look right into people's windows and see what they're up to?"

"Just to look at people in the street," Robert said.

"Oh well! Suppose it'll make a change," Mrs Emmet said. She was always saying things made a change. If you asked her whether she'd had a nice holiday, she wouldn't admit to having enjoyed it or having had good weather, she'd only say, "It was all right. Made a nice change." Johnny said that if she won the pools, which she and her husband did every week, she'd never say she was pleased, she'd only say that it would make a change. Robert wondered if she said that about his accident – "Poor boy, terrible for him to lose his legs like that. Still it makes a change."

It certainly had made a change.

The day drifted by. It was disappointing that there wasn't anything special to look at through the field-glasses, but still he was interested enough to spend the afternoon with them in his hand. He wished more than ever that he could lip-read. He would like to know what the people out there were saying to each other, though probably it would be the sort of conversation he had often overhead in the street and hadn't bothered to listen to. It wasn't likely that any of the regular pedestrians out there could be confiding secrets to each other. Even Scorcher, his spy, would hardly be revealing a terrible spy-ish plot, especially since he very rarely spoke to anyone. What boring lives all these people lived! As the winter afternoon darkened, Robert gave up the binoculars, turned on the light and read. It seemed hard that adventures only happened in books, not on his street.

"See anything interesting today?" his mother asked when she came home that evening.

"Not much. Just ordinary people," Robert said.

"What did you expect? King Kong?" Johnny asked.

"Ha, Ha. Very funny."

"So, what's special about having binoculars to watch ordinary people with?"

"I can see them better. Their expressions. When

they're talking, I can see if it's friendly or if they're quarrelling," Robert said.

"I suppose you'll say that if somebody committed a murder right outside your window, you'd see the murder weapon and how it was done."

"I'd see the murderer, wouldn't I?"

"Who's going to commit a murder here? Nothing ever happens in this rotten place," Clive grumbled.

"I don't want murderers running around here, thank you," Mrs Fox said.

"Well, not a murderer, then. If someone stole a car ..."

"Or broke into the bank ..."

It was quite a thought. For the rest of the evening, Robert's mind ran on the idea of tracking bank robbers, and as he went to sleep he was telling himself the story of how he was watching them gather outside the bank, while he telephoned the police inspector, and circumvented a hideous crime.

Ordinary life wasn't as exciting as what went on in his imagination, but if he was honest, he'd have to admit that the dreaded tutorials enlivened it quite a lot. 'It's odd,' Robert thought, 'how differently things turn out from what you'd imagine.' He'd been angry at first when his mum had told him that he'd got to have a tutor. Then he'd feared making a fool of himself in this new situation. There'd be no chance of hiding what he didn't know or what he hadn't done for homework as there'd been in class. He felt like a specimen laid out for examination, all his lazinesses and the gaps in his knowledge laid bare. But it wasn't like that at all. Molly Feast wasn't interested in showing him up. She only wanted to help him to learn. And it was true, what she'd said, it was quicker, much much quicker being the only pupil, even if he was being taught only for two hours a week.

Mrs Feast didn't teach him at all as he'd been taught at school. She never said, "I want you to read two chapters of this book before I see you again." Instead she asked him, "What do you know about Napoleon?" and when he said, "He was French, wasn't he? Didn't he go to Russia and get stuck in the snow?" She'd laughed at that and said, "I don't suppose Napoleon got stuck himself. His army did, poor things. Did you ever see the film of *War and Peace*?"

He hadn't, of course. She asked, "Have you got a video?" and when he said, No, they hadn't, she said she'd bring hers along one evening and he could watch the film which would tell him something about Napoleon in Russia. It seemed a curious idea, teaching him through showing him videos. For several weeks he didn't feel as if this was teaching at all. Then, gradually, he realised that through getting interested in Napoleon, he'd learned a bit of geography – the countries Napoleon's army had had to get through; a bit of maths – the number of miles they'd covered and the amount of food that had to be carried with them;

and quite a lot about the French way of life, both before and after the emperor's reign.

It wasn't learning as he'd ever experienced it in school. That had never seemed to have much to do with real life. You kept it in a compartment separate from everyday living. As you went into your classroom at school, you opened the compartment and fished out what you needed for the next lesson: Maths. Not bad, but useless. History. Boring, full of names that meant nothing. Geography. Totally forgettable, mostly about places you'd never head of. Science. Watching Mr Bassinger pour coloured liquids from one glass container into another and hoping there'd be an explosion when he heated them up on the burner. R.E. Incomprehensible, he hadn't managed to remember any of it for more than an hour or so.

This sort of learning, he realised with astonishment, was much more like doing a jigsaw puzzle. At first you saw a whole lot of little snippets of knowledge, all different shapes and colours, that didn't seem to have anything to do with each other. And then you began to fit one or two of them together and you could see a picture, much larger than anything you'd imagined, slowly form, and it all started to make sense. So that you saw how it was that all the grandeur of the French court, and the nobles who ruled the country, had to be overthrown in the Revolution. And you saw that when the bloodiness of the Revolution had sickened the people who had started it, there was a place for someone like Napoleon, who wasn't noble (and, he learned, wasn't even properly French), to come along with a different set of rules which the country could accept. Then Napoleon grew too big for his boots and stopped winning his battles, and so he was thrown out in turn and something new took his place.

It was an eye-opener to Robert. He'd always thought of history as dates you were expected to learn. Just as he'd thought of English literature as speeches by Shakespeare and shorter poems by other poets, nothing to do with him, Robert. Instead of which there were books he found he wanted to read, which told him about history and even geography, too. Darwin's voyage in the *Beagle*. *A Tale of Two Cities*. *Robbery Under Arms* (about two brothers who actually lived in Australia and stole cattle and whose father had been one of the convicts transported there). Extraordinary! These things had really happened and not in the long, long ago days when early men lived in caves and wore skins, but only a few grandfathers ago. That was Molly Feast's expression. It made him laugh. But it made him think, too, in a way he never had before.

It didn't take long for him to realise that this was what she wanted him to do. "Don't say what you think I want to hear. Tell me what you feel about it," she sometimes snapped at him. She could be fierce as well as funny. One day she brought Ben, her baby, with her to Robert's lesson. "I'm sorry about Ben, but I haven't anyone to leave him with. If he's troublesome, I'll take him off and come another time," she said. But Ben was no trouble. He walked unsteadily about the room, pushing a plastic tractor around, turning any knobs in sight and trying to balance one brick on top of another. Every now and then he looked at his mother and Robert as if he was comparing what they were doing with his own occupations. He wasn't beautiful; he was a solid child, with a round face and sticking-out ears, but he had a radiant smile. Robert found that he quite liked him. At the end of the hour's lessons, he got down on the floor and built a tower of bricks that was taller than Ben, and he was pleased when Ben

knocked it down and said what Molly interpreted as "again". He asked Molly if she could bring Ben with her another day, but she was firm in her refusal. "I don't want you distracted while you're working with me, and I don't want to have to attend to anything else while I'm here." Robert considered asking his mother to invite Molly and Ben to tea one day, then decided that it would be too much bother. And he didn't want to see Johnny able to carry Ben around on his shoulders, when all he, Robert, could do was sit on the floor and build toy castles out of a child's bricks.

CHAPTER 12

The following week, Sidonie came to see him again.

Robert was astonished. He'd been surprised by her first visit and had not expected that she'd come again. It was half-past four, on a wet, windy December afternoon, and his room was half dark. He'd been reading a book Johnny had brought from the library, but he wasn't really interested and he was half asleep when Johnny opened his door, looked in and said, "Sidonie's here." Robert could tell from his voice that he was equally surprised that she'd come back.

"All right. Tell her to come in," Robert said. At least he was properly dressed this time, though he could never match her. Today she had changed from her schoolclothes and was wearing a bright sweater, with patterned tights showing off her long, shapely legs.

She came in behind Johnny and sat down near Robert without waiting to be asked. She said, "Hi!"

Robert said, "Hi!" too.

"You don't mind my coming to see you again?" Sidonie asked. But she didn't expect an answer. She assumed she'd be welcome. Robert could see that from her expression. Lovely, kind Sidonie, visiting poor crippled Robert. How could he feel anything but gratitude?

Instead he felt angry. He would not reply.

"What've you been doing all day?" she asked next.

"Nothing much. Reading."

Another pause. She picked up his book. *The Mysterious Affair at Styles*.

"Is it good?"

"Not very. It's too easy to tell what's going to happen."

"Can you really?" She opened her eyes wide. "You must be terribly clever. I wouldn't be able to. But I don't read mysteries much."

"What do you read?" Robert asked. He wasn't interested in what she read, but there were such long gaps in the conversation that it seemed as if it might die away altogether.

"I really like romance. I like reading about people getting what they want and being happy. I don't see why people want to read about murders and people being beaten up or starving to death or horrible things like that."

"Because things like that happen," Robert said.

"Well, I don't want to read about them, even if they do."

That seemed to be the end of that topic of conversation.

Remembering what she'd talked about on her last visit, Robert said, "Are you still keen on being an air hostess?"

She looked animated for the first time. "No, I've definitely made up my mind. I'm going to go for modelling. I met this girl who's in one of those schools in London and she says she's sure I'd get a place there. She says half the girls there aren't ... She thinks I'd be just as good as them. She says most of them haven't an idea how to hold themselves or how to wear clothes, they have to be taught everything from scratch. She says I'd be a walk-over. Only I can't go till I'm seventeen, so suppose I'll have to ..."

Her voice ran on. She didn't seem to need any encouragement or comments on what she was saying. Robert allowed his thoughts to drift away. He was surprised at himself. If anyone had told him a year ago that Sidonie Frost would come to sit with him and that he'd be bored out of his mind by her, he wouldn't have believed it. Presently her voice stopped and he heard her complain, "I don't believe you've heard a single word I said."

He said hastily, "Yes, I did." He guessed. "You were talking about being a model."

He'd got it right. She said, "But of course that'd be after I'd got to the top."

"Sounds wonderful," Robert said, guessing again.

"Of course, I don't know if I'll ever make it."

"I'm sure you will."

"Jalda says more than half of them don't. Even if

they're quite good-looking. I expect they're all a lot more glamorous than I am."

He knew that she was waiting for him to tell her that she was wrong, that she'd be the most attractive girl there. But he wouldn't. Instead, he said, "Who's Jalda?"

"I told you. She's this girl who's in the model school ..." She broke off to say, "Goodness! It's nearly five, I'll have to run. I'd no idea it was so late. Sorry, Robert. I'll come again another day."

She was at the door, in a hurry to be off.

When she'd gone, Johnny came into the room. "How'd you get on with Sidonie?"

"She's dead boring," Robert said.

"I wish Jake could hear you say that. He's crazy about her, thinks she's zingy." 'Zingy' was the latest superlative at school.

"He can have her. I can't think why she bothers to come here."

"I know," Johnny said.

"Why does she, then?"

"There's a sort of award for that sort of thing. Social. You know."

"No, I don't. What sort of thing?"

"Visiting hospitals and old people's homes. Cleaning up the canal, that's one project. You put your name down for doing something like that, and you get so many points. Malcolm's doing gardens for pensioners, only because it's winter there's hardly anything to do."

"What's that got to do with Sidonie coming here?"

"Visiting you counts. Timmy told me he heard her ask if it had to be people in hospital, and Mr Grainger said, 'No, it could be in the person's home, if they were ill or disabled or something.'"

It explained a lot, but it made him sick. He was part of Sidonie's charity do-gooding. No wonder she couldn't think of anything to talk about apart from her rotten ambitions. He could just hear her high, rather monotonous voice saying. "Of *course* I went to see poor Robert. I wanted to try to cheer him up. It's so hard on him, being stuck in that dreary little room ..."

"Sorry. After all, she's been twice, hasn't she? I expect she really likes coming," Johnny said.

"No, she doesn't. She's bored stiff. Except when she's talking about being a model," Robert said.

He did not want to see Sidonie again. He said, "Next time she comes, tell her I can't see her. Say I'm on the loo or something. Just make sure she doesn't come back."

"What about Anthea?" Johnny asked.

"Does she come because of this award thing?"

"Don't know. Shouldn't think so."

"Find out, will you? And if that is why, I don't want to see her either."

It was the Thursday of the week after Sidonie's visit

that something worth watching did happen in the street below Robert's window.

Looking across the road he saw a man getting money out of the cash dispenser. Behind him there was a small queue; another man with a thin pony-tail hanging over his coat collar; behind him two young women, one of them dark, and striking, in a short scarlet jacket worn over long black leggings; behind them a middle-aged man in a black coat and striped trousers. Robert decided that he was a dentist. As he watched, the first man withdrew his money and left. The man with the pony-tail had difficulties dealing with the dispenser. Robert saw him punch his number twice before he apparently gave up and walked away. Then the two girls stood on the pavement for a long time; they seemed to be arguing about something; perhaps they weren't sure how the machine worked. Robert saw the middle-aged man behind them become impatient. He spoke to them sharply once or twice and at length the dark girl punched her PIN number and put out her hand to take the money.

Robert saw now that the pony-tailed man was back. He suddenly pushed against the girl so that she staggered sideways and, in that instant, he snatched the notes and ran off. Robert saw the second girl try to take hold of his coat, but he had pulled it out of her grasp and run down the High Street and out of Robert's sight in the time that it took the first girl to

pull herself upright again. She screamed. There seemed to be a white sea of faces turned towards her. People had run to shop doors to look, and a man came out of the bank and stood at its double doors, asking everyone what had happened.

It was like, Robert thought, seeing the disturbance inside an ant hill. All the passers-by collected round the bank doors, while another man and woman came out and helped the dark girl inside. Five minutes later a police car came wailing up to stop with a screech of brakes and two policemen jumped out and also went into the bank. The crowd on the pavement was growing larger as more pedestrians came up to join it and to ask what had happened. Presently the policemen came out and began to question some of the people and Robert was interested to notice that several of the bystanders seemed to be talking busily, as if they could give accounts of what had happened, although he knew they'd arrived long after the event.

It was maddening. Here he was, exactly opposite the scene of the crime, uniquely equipped to have seen everything in detail with his binoculars; he might even have been able to observe some distinguishing marks on the criminal. But he'd seen practically nothing. If only he'd been prepared, he'd have had the glasses to his eyes, he'd have made a mental note of anything which might help the police to catch the thief. As it was, he couldn't contribute anything new;

the two girls had probably had a better view of the man than he had. He hadn't even noticed what the man was wearing, all he could remember was the incongruous pony-tail. He could have kicked himself, and as he thought this, he thought also that he couldn't even do that. He was a cripple. He couldn't kick anyone.

It took time for the crowd to disperse. Someone came out of the bank and stuck a piece of white paper over the cash dispenser. Through the field-glasses Robert read what was written on the paper: DISPENSER TEMPORARILY OUT OF USE. About a quarter of an hour later the two girls came out of the bank and were driven away in the police car. Soon the pavement was no more crowded than it usually was at midday on Thursday. The school crocodile returned, with sleek damp hair and dripping towels. Everything seemed to have gone back to normal. Robert sat at the window and fumed. He'd wanted something exciting to happen, he'd imagined that he'd be part of it, somehow or other. Now it had happened and he hadn't even observed it properly. He felt as useless as his legs.

It was worse that afternoon.

"Rob? You see that snatch?" Johnny asked the moment he was back from school.

"What snatch?" He pretended not to understand.

"Outside the bank. Some girl was getting money

out of the cash machine and a man came along and grabbed the notes before she'd got hold of them. Right opposite. You must have seen it!"

"I saw there was something happening. There was a whole crowd of people."

"I was sure you'd be able to tell the police what the man looked like, now you've got those glasses. Didn't you see anything?" Johnny asked, disappointed.

"Not really. I hadn't got the glasses where I could reach them," Robert lied.

"Shame! Still, now he's got away with it once, he may try it again, and another time you'd see him properly."

"He wouldn't try it at the same place again. He'd know people'd be on the look-out for him here," Robert said, angry with Johnny for saying what he was feeling himself.

In spite of believing what he'd told Johnny, Robert did keep an extra careful watch for a few days. It was just possible that the thief would try it on again. But nothing happened. It occurred to him that he ought to tell the police what he had managed to see, but he persuaded himself that it wouldn't be any use. He did not want to admit to anyone that he had wasted the chance to be a vital witness to a crime, conveniently committed right under his window. It was sickening. It made him feel even more useless and hopeless than before.

CHAPTER 13

He was not pleased when Anthea appeared at the door of his room at the end of Monday afternoon.

"Would you rather I went away again? Johnny said he wasn't sure you'd want a visitor."

Which meant that Johnny hadn't discovered the reason for Anthea's visits. Robert said grudgingly, "It's all right. I mean, you can come in."

She shut the door behind her and came over to his chair.

"I brought you this." She put it on the table by him.

"I know it's shabby. It's secondhand. They had a sort of jumble sale at the empty shop round the corner and I saw this and I remembered you said you liked his books, so I thought you wouldn't mind that it isn't new."

It was certainly a well-thumbed paperback, but it was by his almost favourite writer and he'd never read it. He said, embarrassed, "Thanks. That's great."

"You haven't got it?"

"Never heard of it."

"I hope it's good."

Still embarrassed, he said, "I should pay you for it."

Now he'd made her feel bad. She'd turned red. "No! It's a present."

"You sure?" How stupid could he get? "Well. Thanks a lot."

There was a pause.

"I'd better go," she said.

"Not unless you want to." He must find out if she was coming out of a sense of duty, or to win an award, like Sidonie. He said, "Johnny says some people at school are going in for a sort of award scheme."

She said, "Are they? Johnny is?"

"Not Johnny. Sidonie."

"Oh, her. She may be. I don't know."

"But you're not?"

"I'm not the sort that wins awards," she said.

"You're not in for it, then?"

"What's the award for?"

"It's social." He couldn't bring himself to say 'do-gooding'.

"Social?"

"Visiting hospitals and things like that."

"It's stupid. You shouldn't have to have an award for that."

"But if people wouldn't do it without?"

"Then they'd better not do it at all. It's cheating. It's like pretending you're that sort of person when really you aren't." She was quite stirred up. He didn't know what to say. She was looking at him, then she said, "You thought that was why I came to see you?"

"No ... Not really ..."

"You did!"

"I couldn't help wondering."

"Well, it wasn't. I'm not like that."

"All right."

"I'm going now," she said, and left before he'd thought of anything more to say. Unsatisfactory.

It was cold and getting colder. On Tuesday morning the people Robert saw in the High Street had muffled themselves up: scarves round their necks, thick coats, woolly caps pulled down over their ears. The younger women wore boots and short padded jackets, below which their legs looked long and spindly in patterned tights. Mr Moon was huddled in a tattered check coat, two sizes too large for him, and Scorcher appeared in a motorist's leather cap with earflaps and huge wrap-around tinted spectacles as if he expected snow. Mrs Bags did not appear at all. Peter, the blind man, looked thinner and more helpless than usual, wearing the same clothes he'd had in the autumn, still feeling his slow way along the crowded pavements. Robert saw how the hurrying people pushed him around. Through his binoculars he could see the lost expression on Peter's face and he raged, "Why don't they help him? Why doesn't someone stop and take him across the road?"

Just then, someone did. It wasn't one of the regulars, but a man in a khaki raincoat and a cloth cap. Robert trained the binoculars on him, and saw round spectacles perched on a long, pointed nose above a bristly chin. Nothing out of the ordinary. When the man had escorted Peter to the further pavement, he returned to where he'd been before. It had been kindness then, that had made him cross over. Now he was looking into Mr Jenkins' window, standing next to Scorcher, who often stood there for minutes at a time, though he never seemed to go inside. No money for butcher's meat, probably. Robert saw the man say something to Scorcher but Scorcher didn't answer, he scuttled away. Robert had noticed before that Scorcher didn't like being talked to. Robert had never seen him in conversation with anyone. He hadn't gone far, though. Now he was back again, hovering on the other side of the bank by the door of the supermarket. 'Perhaps', Robert thought, 'he's really a bank robber, waiting for an opportunity to go in and stage a hold-up.' It didn't seem likely, but it would explain the leather cap and the tinted glasses. But, Robert decided sadly, Scorcher didn't look like the sort of man who would ever do a risky thing like that.

Mr Moon was there now, entangled in his dog's lead, as usual. While he was trying to free himself, the helpful man spoke to him too, and Mr Moon, who was obviously sociable, answered. They talked for quite a time. Mr Moon was gesticulating and pointing; perhaps the helpful man was asking the way somewhere. Then at last the dog's lead was untangled

and Mr Moon moved off. The helpful man took another look in the butcher's window and then strolled off, past the bank to the supermarket and disappeared through its glass door. Robert didn't feel sufficiently interested in him to give him a name. He'd probably never see him again.

Another delivery van drew up outside the supermarket. Those vans were at it all day. Robert had counted fifteen, one day. Until he'd been stationed at his window, he'd had no idea people got through food at such a rate. A long black car was stopping near the van. The Rolls. It must be half-past ten already, and there was Eddie's dad getting out and holding the back passenger door open for Mrs Braithwaite. She was wearing a long fur coat and a little round hat of the same soft brown fur. Robert saw her trip into the bank on the accustomed high heels. Would she take more money out today because it was nearly Christmas? If the pony-tailed man had known about Mrs Braithwaite, he might have thought it worth his while to snatch her handbag as she came out, rather than whatever money the girl had drawn from the dispenser.

Eddie's dad stood by the car. Robert supposed that he knew exactly how long Mrs Braithwaite would be inside the building, and had calculated that it wasn't worthwhile sitting in the driver's seat. Because it was so cold, he was pacing the pavement, but never out of reach of that beautiful car. Eddie had told Johnny that his dad really loved the car. "My mum says he'd rather have the car than her, he never thinks about anything else." Well, who wouldn't? It was beautiful, and Eddie said it could go something like a hundred and twenty miles an hour, only his dad wouldn't ever go that fast, he didn't think it was safe, unless you were on a proper speedtrack.

The crocodile from the primary school was straggling along the pavement. Either they were early or Mrs Braithwaite had been later than usual, they didn't generally overlap. She came out of the bank just as Robert thought this, and threaded her way through the small children, who were swinging their satchels and bags, too busy chattering to look where they were going. Eddie's dad opened the car door and Mrs Braithwaite got in. Robert saw one or two of the boys in the crocodile pointing out the car to one another before it slid silently away.

Robert would have given a lot to have a ride in that car. He remembered his dad's expression – "That'd cost you an arm and a leg." He'd lost two legs, hadn't he? But he'd never get inside that car.

He noticed then the helpful man who had taken blind Peter across the road. He must have come out of the supermarket without Robert noticing. He was carrying one of their red plastic bags. He seemed not to be in a hurry to go anywhere, and Robert wondered why. It wasn't the weather for standing about. Just then a nondescript grey Ford drew up by the pavement and the helpful man opened the front passenger door and got in. The car disappeared in an easterly direction. Boring, boring. Robert sighed.

He picked up the book that Anthea had brought the day before, meaning only to glance at the beginning. Two hours later he was astonished to find that he'd read half of it and Mrs Emmet was carrying in his midday meal.

He finished the book that afternoon. It was good, one of the author's best. He thought that when he saw Anthea again, he'd tell her he'd enjoyed it. He hadn't been very grateful when she'd given it to him and he'd probably hurt her feelings by suggesting that her visits to him were like Sidonie's, made with an award in view. She probably wouldn't come back.

It was a long afternoon; sleety rain began to fall and darkness came early. Robert felt depressed and cross. When Johnny came back from school, Robert said, "Did you tell Sidonie?"

"Tell her what?"

"That she needn't bother to come back."

"Haven't seen her all day."

"What about Anthea?"

"Haven't seen her either."

He wondered if Anthea would come back.

That evening he asked his mother, "Do they do men's hair at your place?"

"Not much. Sometimes one of the boss's friends comes in and he'll do a cut for him. And little boys, their mothers bring them."

"But not just anyone?"

"People don't often come in off the street without an appointment, if that's what you mean."

It was what he'd meant. He'd wondered if she could tell him about Scorcher or Peter or Mr Moon. Though now he thought of it, none of them looked as if they'd have money to spend on haircuts. Trimmed their own hair with nail scissors more likely.

"Why do you want to know?" his mother asked.

"Doesn't matter."

"Anyone particular you wanted to know about?"

He couldn't tell her. It would sound ridiculous.

"Do you see the same people out there in the street? So that you'd recognise them?" his mum was asking.

He said, "Some." Then, "Not often. There's the kids from the school and that woman with plastic bags. Mostly I don't remember them."

"It's a busy street," his mother said.

"I see that woman Eddie's dad drives for. Who doesn't have her hair done at 'Top Dressing'."

His mother laughed. "How am I supposed to know all the women who don't come into the shop?"

"Johnny says she's married to a millionaire. She has a Rolls."

"You asked about her before. Anyone else?"

"There's a blind man. Young. And an old man with a dog."

"There must be a lot more."

"I only get to know them if they come past a lot."

"I wish it was more interesting for you," Robert's mother said.

"It's more interesting now that I've got the binoculars."

She looked more cheerful when he said that. "I'm glad. And Mrs Feast's done you good. I'll have to think of something she'd like for Christmas."

Robert said, "You don't have to go and spend a lot of money on a present for her, mum. I'm sure she'd like it if it was just a card."

"The boss might let me have something from the salon at cost price. They have lovely perfumes. I'll see."

Robert hugged his own secret. Molly Feast had told him once that she liked trying new recipes and he'd got Johnny to go and look for a brand new cookery book. A paperback, he couldn't have afforded anything more. Johnny had come back from the bookshop, flushed with success and with a book called *Food for Feasts and Festivals*. Robert had no idea whether the recipes inside the bright covers were any good, but the title made it just the right present. He looked forward to giving it to Molly next time she came to see him.

CHAPTER 14

Then, suddenly, it was the Tuesday of Christmas week. Thursday would be Christmas Day. Mrs Fox started work early and warned Robert and the others that she'd be back late. "Everyone wants to have a hair-do before The Day. We'll have to have supper late this evening. I'll do what I can to get away, but it's always difficult at this time of year."

It was a long, dark morning. Johnny and Clive were out with their friends, and Robert was left to himself, except for Mrs Emmet's occasional visits to his room. He spent an hour or so wrapping up presents for his mum and his brothers. He hadn't been able to choose them himself, of course: Mum had bought the boys' and Johnny had bought Mum's. It was disappointing. He knew so many things he'd have liked to be able to give her: a really good handbag, some sort of jewellery – a brooch or ear-rings, a new radio, a winter coat. But now he couldn't earn money by doing odd jobs, all he had to spend was his pocket money, and that was given him by his mum. 'So whatever I give her is really only like handing back the money she's given me,' Robert thought, depressed.

He reckoned there wouldn't be much to watch today, apart from people carrying home their

Christmas trees and their turkeys. He was half on the watch for the crocodile of kids going swimming, when he remembered that the holidays had begun. He'd seen a procession of small children, carrying bright, badly painted banners, cluttering up the pavement the Friday before, when they'd been let out an hour early to celebrate the end of term. Now the street below his window was crowded with people doing their last-minute shopping. Everyone seemed to be clutching parcels, carrying bulging plastic bags, all in a good-humoured sort of hurry. If he looked through the binoculars, he could actually see their lips forming the words "Happy Christmas" as they passed or, often, bumped into each other. He saw a woman in a hat like a coal-scuttle give money to Mrs Bags, who was standing outside the supermarket and smiling away as usual. He saw Mr Moon go into the butcher's. Perhaps for once he was going to buy a bone for his dog. Scorcher scuttled into view, glancing, also as usual, from left to right and from right to left as he moved along the pavement. He saw Peter and, walking by him, a girl, who was taking him across the road. He looked again and saw that the girl was Anthea. He wondered if she was coming to visit him, but although she was now on his side of the road, he did not hear the doorbell ring and he lost sight of her.

He was looking for people he recognised. Scorcher was now leaning up against the butcher's window, as if he needed support. When he took a step or two, Robert saw that he was indeed unsteady on his feet. But he was still looking around in that suspicious way of his. Mr Moon had disappeared. But Robert did see the helpful man who had taken blind Peter across the road the previous week. He was just standing, this time, leaning up against the supermarket window, sometimes looking in at the array of bottles, sometimes looking around. He was even more wrapped up against the cold today, with not only the cloth cap pulled down to his eyebrows, but also a muffler round the lower half of his face. Perhaps he was waiting for the car to pick him up, as it had done before. Robert put his face right up against his window and peered along the street, and as he did so, the grey Ford came into view, driving slowly. Looking for the helpful man? But this time it came to a stop bang outside the bank doors and the helpful man did not move to get in. Instead he jerked his head, as if he was communicating with the car's driver, then turned and continued to study the labels on the bottles of wine.

'Eddie's dad won't be pleased when he sees his place has been taken,' Robert thought. He watched two men get out of the shabby car. He'd assumed that they were going into the bank, or perhaps the butcher's or the supermarket. He expected them at least to go over to speak to the helpful man: since they'd just got out of the car that had picked him up before, they must know each other. But instead they strolled off, not apparently in a hurry, towards Walter's sandwich bar on the corner. Perhaps they had just stopped for sandwiches or a cup of tea.

More people streamed along the pavement. Mrs Bags was still there, dawdling as usual and holding up the more energetic pedestrians. Robert saw Molly Feast with Ben, who was wearing a scarlet snowsuit with white fur trimmings that made him look like a very small Father Christmas. Molly pushed the baby buggy into the butcher's. 'Picking up her turkey,' Robert thought, but it would take some time. There was a queue of at least five people ahead of her.

Next, Robert saw the Rolls. Eddie's dad drove up at his usual even pace and parked just in front of the shabby grey car. Robert saw Mrs Braithwaite get out, in grey fur today, and trip across to the bank door, where she disappeared.

The next thing was decidedly odd. The shabby car backed, then pulled out and went fast along the street to the right. Sixty seconds later it had come back from the opposite direction and pulled in immediately in front of the Rolls. Eddie's dad, standing near the rear end of the car and talking animatedly to a passer-by, didn't appear to have noticed this manoeuvre.

The two men had come back from Walter's café now and were standing outside the bank, by the cash dispenser. And the helpful man had apparently finished studying the supermarket window and was on the other side of the bank's door, glancing inside. All three of them looked as if they were waiting for something to happen.

Perhaps it was this air of expectancy that made Robert reach for his binoculars. Through the glasses he studied the three men. The two by the dispenser he'd never seen before. They were ordinary, remarkably ordinary if that is possible. Then he trained the sights on the helpful man. The helpful man was standing still. As Robert looked at him, he patted the right-hand pocket of his thick jacket, and for a split second Robert saw the outline of what the pocket contained. Both the gesture and the outline were familiar. Robert had seen them a hundred times on television dramas. The helpful man was making sure that his pocket still held his gun.

Then Robert knew what they were waiting for. They were going to attack Mrs Braithwaite when she came out of the bank and snatch her handbag with all the money she'd just drawn from her account. That was why they were grouped like that between the bank doors and the waiting car. And the car's engine was running. And any moment now, Mrs Braithwaite would be coming out.

Robert had to think quickly. Worse, he'd have to act before he'd had time to work anything out. He could open his window and shout, but would anyone hear him above the noise of traffic and the Salvation Army band playing 'While Shepherds Watched ...' on the corner? Or if they could hear, would anyone believe him? Before he knew that he had made any decision, he was out of the chair by the window and had crutched his way into the passage outside his door. No time to go down the stairs using the banister and one crutch as he'd been taught by Frankie. He sat on the top step and slithered, uncomfortably and dangerously, but quickly, down to the hallway at the bottom, where his wheelchair stood. He was breathing fast and he could actually hear his heart drumming in his ears. He had no time. Mrs Braithwaite might by now be outside the bank, might have had her bag snatched from her. Somehow he managed to get himself into the chair. Next he had to open the front door. It meant that he had to lean forward at a dangerous angle, holding on to a chair arm with one hand, desperately trying to unlock the door with the other hand. It took him what seemed like minutes, but when he got out on to the pavement, the grey car was still there and so were the three men.

He had meant to turn along the pavement as far as the pedestrian crossing, but he saw the bank door open and he knew that he wouldn't make it. He shot his wheelchair into the road.

He heard the screeching of more than one set of brakes and the grinding crash as the car which had just missed him was jammed by the one behind. Several people were shouting. There was a lot of bad language. But he was on the further side of the road, and now he saw that it wasn't Mrs Braithwaite's handbag the three men were after, it was her, herself. One of the two waiting men had caught hold of her and had a hand over her mouth and was dragging her towards the grey car, while the other had produced a gun and was sweeping it around, pointed at the people standing by. Somebody screamed, and Robert saw that the third man, the 'helpful' man, was holding something bright, something scarlet as fresh blood in front of him. He was holding his gun to the head of a terrified baby. He had snatched Ben out of his buggy. He was threatening to kill Ben.

Robert had to make the quickest decision of his life. He made for the figures struggling down the

pavement, and for the first time was grateful that the wheelchair was heavy.

He thought that he had brought Mrs Braithwaite down on the pavement, then the impact with her and with the man holding her knocked him out of his chair. There was a split second in which he saw that the man had lost his hat. A huge, gleaming bald head shone above him like a monstrous pink moon. Then he knew he was falling, and felt that he ought to be able to help himself but couldn't. Then nothing.

He was conscious of a sharp pain on one side of his head. There was also a duller pain in his shoulder and upper arm. He couldn't remember how they had got there.

"What?" Robert said to no one in particular.

"It's all right. Just lie still, old man," an unfamiliar voice said.

He opened his eyes. He was lying on a pavement, and there were people standing all round him. A woman was kneeling by his side and holding his wrist. 'Taking his pulse,' he thought. 'Why?'

"I'm all right," he said, not feelling it.

"Ambulance's coming," she said.

"Could have broken his arm," another voice said.

"Ben?" Robert said.

"What's that?"

"Is Ben all right?"

"The baby? He's all right, his mum's taken him home. Waited to make sure you were okay, though."

"Ambulance should be here soon."

"A nasty crack on his head."

"Might have been a bad accident when he went into the road like that. Didn't stop to look at the traffic." A complaining voice spoke.

"If he hadn't sent the chair into them, they'd have got away with it."

"Brave boy. Could have been shot."

Robert tried to sit up, but his head hurt too much. "What happened?" he asked.

"Lost his memory. Probably concussion," a woman said.

"Nonsense! If you'd gone on to the pavement head first like that, you might not be able to remember exactly what got you there."

"What did happen?" Robert asked again.

"You came shooting across the road in your chair and went straight into Mrs Braithwaite and the man who was trying to take her off. Knocked them both off their balance, gave Mr Scott here the chance to get the gun off the man holding the baby. Professional sort of tackle he used, pleasure to see it."

"There was another man," Robert said, still confused.

"He went off as soon as he saw what was happening. Ran like a rabbit that knows there's a ferret after it."

"He got away?"

"Not for long, he won't have. We all had a good look at him. The one in the car got away, drove off as soon as he saw there was nothing doing."

"Mrs Braithwaite? She all right?" Robert asked.

"Bit shaken. Only to be expected. Her driver took her off home."

"I'd like to go home," Robert said.

"Ambulance is coming."

"I don't need an ambulance. I live here. There. The other side of the street."

"You'll have to go to hospital for a check-up first. That was quite a bang you had on the pavement. If they say you're all right, they'll bring you back before you know it."

It was not nearly as quick as that. Robert had to spend more than two hours in the casualty department of the hospital while doctors felt his head and his shoulder, peered into his eyes with small bright lights, put him under the X-ray machine and asked innumerable questions. Meanwhile he was brought cups of tea by hurried nurses who called him "dear" and never asked him to do anything, even putting a thermometer under his tongue or telling them his age and his address, without adding "for me" to the request. "Open your mouth for me, will you?" "Just slip your arm out of your jumper for me, will you?" "Here's your aspirin, just swallow it down in the water, for me, will you?" When all the tests were finished and he was reported to be bruised – "You're going to have a wonderful black eye in a day or two" – but to have no bones broken and was probably not concussed after all, Robert was told they were sending him home. In the ambulance, of course. He was surprised they didn't say, "You can go home now, for me."

Before he actually left, his mother arrived. When she'd been reassured that he was all right, the questions began.

"I don't understand. They said you were mixed up in a kidnap attempt. How could you be? And the wheelchair's damaged, we'll have to pay for it to be mended."

"I saw them from the window. They'd parked in

front of the Rolls."

"Saw who? And I don't see what the parking's got to do with it."

"So it couldn't go after them. Only I thought it was going to be another robbery."

"And how did you get downstairs, anyway? Do try to explain properly."

He tried to tell the story in the way it had happened, but he wasn't very successful.

"I still don't see how you knew what those men were waiting for."

"I didn't, really. I thought they'd just snatch her bag."

"Whose bag? You said, 'the Rolls'. Whose Rolls? Why was anyone parking a Rolls around here this morning?"

"Mum, I told you! Mrs Braithwaite. Eddie's dad drives her."

Before long the police had arrived and asked Robert about every detail, what he had noticed about the three men and the grey car, and what had made him suspect that they were up to no good. Later, the doorbell kept ringing and there was a stream of neighbours and friends wanting to see him. Robert was so tired, he couldn't really attend properly to what they asked or what they said. He also found it confusing that most of the visitors seemed to think he'd been rather a hero, while his mother was divided between pride in what he'd done and horror at his going down the stairs alone, and even more, when neighbours described his mad rush across the busy road, at the risks he'd taken. Worse still, she knew now that two of the men had had guns.

It wasn't till the next day, Christmas Eve, that he really understood. Johnny had got the whole story sorted out.

"The police have got three of the men. And they think they'll get the driver soon. They've got the car. They say one of the men must have been hanging around for weeks to make sure they'd know just how to get Mrs Braithwaite. They say they might have brought it off if you hadn't crashed into them like that. It was really brave of you. You might have got shot."

"I was so mad when I saw that man with Ben, I didn't think about the gun."

"Why didn't you go for him, then?"

"I thought if I did, he might let the gun off by accident. And if I managed to stop the other one from taking Mrs Braithwaite off, he'd have to let Ben go so that he could get away himself. Anyway, everything happened so quickly I didn't have time to worry."

"Eddie says you'll probably get a reward. Mr Braithwaite's a millionaire."

This was an agreeable thought, but Robert then had another idea.

"I saw a movie on telly last week where a man got some people to kidnap his wife because he was fed up with her and he wanted to marry someone else."

"If Mr Braithwaite's like that, he'll probably try again," Johnny said.

"It'd be just my luck if he is."

"Eddie says Mum needn't worry about the chair, because he says Mr Braithwaite will pay for it to be mended."

"That'll make Mum feel a lot better."

"And guess what! You know that old man who sort of creeps around, looking over his shoulder all the time?"

Scorcher, Robert said in his inside mind. Aloud he said, "Yes, I know."

"Guess what he was before he retired? Scott, he's called."

"A spy," Robert said, not quite seriously.

"How did you know?" Johnny asked, more impressed by this than by anything else that Robert had done.

"He isn't really? I mean, is he?"

"Worked for M.I.5 in the war. That's how he came to know how to tackle that man with the gun."

"That's fantastic!" Robert said.

"Thought you'd like it. I say, Rob, your eye's going the most peculiar colours. It's violet round the edge. Does it hurt?"

"Don't ask stupid questions," Robert said, in a perfectly friendly way.

CHAPTER 15

Christmas morning. Robert's mum was making a meal that might be late breakfast or dinner; by the smells that wafted along the passage it was going to be good. Johnny and Clive were in and out of the kitchen and Robert's room. The doorbell rang more than once and he heard the voices of Johnny's and Clive's friends, who had either come to exhibit their Christmas presents or to ask about the attempted kidnap. Robert did not want to have to talk about it. His head ached and he still felt bewildered by the speed at which everything had happened. Even when Molly Feast and her husband came in with Ben to bring him a video machine as a thank-you present for saving Ben, nothing seemed quite real. He was glad when, in the middle of a really embarrassing thank-you exchange between Molly and himself, Ben started screaming and had to be taken away. "Over excitement," Mr Feast said and hurried them out.

Later that morning there was the giving of gifts. Again, Robert felt a pang when his mother unwrapped the scarf which was his present for her. Johnny had chosen well, it was really pretty, but it wasn't anything out of the ordinary. He'd wanted to give her something she'd never have been able to get for herself. She kissed him. "It's lovely, Robert. It'll make me look as good as your Mrs Braithwaite."

"All right, Mum, don't go on about it."

"Perhaps I should have kept the binoculars till now. Then I'd have had something good to give you – "

"But then Rob wouldn't have seen that the man had a gun, and he mightn't have done anything about the kidnap," Johnny said.

"I wish he hadn't," Robert's mother said, looking worried.

"Mum! You mean you wish she had been kidnapped?"

"No-o ... But I'd rather Robert hadn't had anything to do with it."

"Why not? Think! He might get a big reward."

"I shan't," Robert said. Nothing so lucky would happen to him.

"Well, look at him. All bruised and shaken. It isn't good for him. And the chair's going to need mending. And I don't like the idea that those men know who he is. They might decide to take it out on him for stopping them."

"They'll be in prison for years. By the time they come out Rob'll look different," Johnny said.

"I'll grow a beard, then they won't have a clue who I am," Robert said.

"But you'll still ..." his mother said. She didn't finish the sentence. Robert knew that she'd been going to say, "You'll still be in a wheelchair, you'll still be a cripple." First he was sad, then he was angry. He said, "I'll be walking properly by then. You'll see."

It was the first time he'd ever said it.

The doorbell rang again. Johnny went to answer it. When he came back he had news. "That was Eddie. He says his dad says Mr Braithwaite's coming to see you. Not today, because of it being Christmas, but soon. Eddie's dad says Mr Braithwaite thinks you're terrific, the way you saved Mrs Braithwaite, and he's going to do something about it. Give you something or do something for you. What d'you think it'll be?"

"How do I know? I don't know anything about him."

"It could be a reward. A lot of money. I told you, he's a millionaire."

"It could be a chiming clock," Robert said.

"Why a clock? What for?"

"That's what they give old men when they leave a job they've been in for years. It's called the Golden Handshake. Only it isn't ever gold."

"But you're not leaving a job. And you're not old. I think it'll be money. Suppose he gave you a thousand pounds?"

"Suppose he doesn't. He wouldn't give me anything like that."

"He might. Eddie's dad says he's crazy about her. Mrs Braithwaite. Eddie's dad says he hired a man to look after her."

"He didn't do it very well, did he?" Robert said.

"He did get one of the men with the gun."

"Who did?"

"Her minder. Scott, he's called."

"Scorcher was her minder?" Robert said, astonished.

"Eddie's dad thinks he was a bit drunk yesterday, that's why he wasn't on the look-out for trouble."

"He didn't look too steady on his legs," Robert agreed. So that was why Scorcher was always hanging around and peering this way and that. He was not only really an ex-spy, he was also Mrs Braithwaite's minder. Robert wondered if any of the other regulars were somehow involved in the incident.

He wasn't hungry for their Christmas dinner. He was surprisingly tired, and found that he had slept through most of the thriller on the television. In the early evening, while he was waiting for his mother to bring him tea and a slice of the Christmas cake she prided herself on, he allowed himself to wonder whether Mr Braithwaite would really offer him a reward. Suppose he did, how much would it be? He played around with Johnny's suggestion of a thousand pounds. It would be wonderful if his mum didn't have to work so hard, and if he could have one of the really up-to-date wheelchairs that did everything by electronics. But no amount of money was going to bring him back his two independent legs.

It was a short afternoon, but crowded. Half the neighbourhood "Just had to drop in" on their after-dinner walks. Robert was not best pleased to see Sidonie, full of enthusiasm. "Oh, Robert! You're a hero! I think you're wonderful! I can't think how you managed." Robert was embarrassed and short with her, but even so it took a good ten minutes to get her out. His mum, who had never seen her before, came in when Sidonie had at last left, to say, "That's a lovely girl. Who is she?"

"Someone from school," Robert said.

"Is she a special friend?" his mum dared to ask.

"She's not a friend at all. I don't want to see her if she comes again." So much for the future pin-up girl.

Later, when it was dark, Johnny put his head round Robert's door to say, "Anthea's here. Want her to come in?"

"She can if she likes," Robert said.

Anthea didn't come further than the doorway. "Your mother says you're tired. I won't stay. I just wanted to say I think what you did on Tuesday was great."

Robert found he was quite sorry when she went away so quickly.

He wasn't pleased when there was yet another ring of the doorbell. A heavy step in the passage, then a man's voice joining in the hubbub. It wouldn't be Mr Braithwaite today. It could possibly be Eddie's dad, with a message. Or Mr Robertson, who had been a friend of Mum's father and who came round to see them at Christmas and for Mum's birthday, bringing her flowers or chocolates. But he was deaf and boomed, so that you could hear every word he said, all over the flat. It didn't sound like him. Now, Johnny and Clive were joining in the conversation, laughing, excited. He could hear Mum trying to quiet them down. She was saying something about him – "Remember Robert's in there." Was it bad news that she'd have to break it to him gently? Johnny and Clive's voices didn't sound like that. He could have used his crutches to get himself painfully and slowly out of his room and to the kitchen to join in, but he didn't like strangers seeing him fumbling around. Besides this, the strange voice reminded him of someone he didn't want to think about.

There were feet coming along the passage. More than one person. His mother's and another's. His mum came very quickly into the room. She said, "Robert! It's –" but she didn't have time to finish before the person behind her pushed past and came over to Robert. He sat down beside him and couldn't speak.

"Dad!" Robert said.

"I came ...."

"He's come for Christmas," his wife said.

"Dad? You going to stay?"

"Sort of. Not here. Not far off. I'll explain."

"Dad! Did you hear what Robert did on Tuesday?"
Johnny was saying.

"It was a kidnap and Robert knocked them down ..."
That was Clive trying to get the news in first.

"... and her husband's a millionaire and he's going
to give Rob something for saving her ..."

"They think the minder was drunk or he'd have
stopped it. But he did get one of the men with a gun ..."

"And there was a terrible crash outside here,
because Rob got across the road just in front of a car ..."

"I can't understand a word you're saying. Don't all
talk at once. Let Rob tell me what happened."

It took time. Robert found that Johnny and Clive
knew a great deal more than he did about what had
happened outside the bank. But he was the only one

who could tell what had made him suspicious and how he'd got down the stairs.

Everyone was talking at once. Mrs Fox took charge. "Johnny! Clive! You come with me to the kitchen. Lenny, you can have your coffee in here with Robert. Who'd think it was still Christmas?" She pushed the two younger boys out of the room, leaving Robert alone with his father.

"I didn't get your letter till last month," Robert's dad said.

"What letter? I didn't write to you," Robert said.

"You did. About playing in the team."

"Oh, that!" Was it really only last summer? It seemed a thousand years ago.

"I'm sorry I couldn't get here to see you play."

"That was when I had the accident," Robert said, "Mum told me."

They looked at each other. Robert said quickly, "Don't, Dad. It's not so bad. They said I was lucky it wasn't higher up, or I wouldn't have been able to use my arms or anything."

"You can't walk at all?" his father asked.

"Not properly. Not by myself, without a crutch or something."

"But you will be able to?"

"Frankie says if I try I'll be able to get about on elbow crutches."

"Well, then!"

"It's so boring," Robert said.

"You go to the hospital? They're giving you treatment?"

"Three times a week. But I don't seem to get any better."

"I'll make sure you do. I'm going to go with you whenever I can, and if you don't put some muscle into it, I'll fix you good and proper."

This sounded more like the Dad he'd known. Robert asked, "Have you come back for good, Dad?"

"I'm not going to live here. It wouldn't work. Your mum agrees to that. But I've got to get another job. I'm getting too old for diving. I'm going to be in Thames Ditton. Training youngsters. Not too bad. I'll be over here as often as I can manage. It's not that far. I could come to supper and get back before night."

"But you're here for today?"

"Told you, I'm back for Christmas," Robert's dad said.

"Eats!" Johnny said at the door, holding a tray.

"I'll take it. You go back to Clive and your mum. Now then, Rob. You tell me how you come to be stopping kidnappers at your age. I reckon if you can do that when you're in a wheelchair, there'll be no holding you once you're out and about again with your old dad."